Odd Thoughts

by

G.W. Renshaw

CALGARY, ALBERTA
JAVARI PRESS
Publishers

2014

Odd Thoughts

JAVARI PRESS,
CALGARY, ALBERTA, CANADA.
HTTP://WWW.JAVARIPRESS.CA/

First paperback edition, November 2014.
Cover art from j4p4n and johnny_automatic on openclipart.org

Library and Archives Canada Cataloguing in Publication:

Renshaw, G. W., 1955-, author
    Odd thoughts / by G.W. Renshaw.

Short stories.
ISBN 978-1-895487-04-6 (pbk.)

I. Title.

PS8635.E5785O33 2014   C813'.6   C2014-903404-0

Set in Gentium Book Basic
Printed in the United States of America

Gods are So Unreasonable

"That's a lot of effort for someone who wants to die."

"Where are you? Please, help me!"

"Why don't you help yourself?"

"I can't. I'm hurt." I was starting to sound like a whiny five-year old, but I couldn't help it. "I need help."

"You certainly do. Where are you going to get it?"

I looked around but couldn't see anyone. Movement in the tree caught my eye; the leafy face was back. The mouth seemed to move in synch with the words which seemed only slightly peculiar at the time. I thought, *how can the leaves be moving if there's no wind?* I must have been delirious. Maybe it's not just those who have been manhandled by Orcs who think that talking trees are normal.

"Please, I need help."

"So you say. Again, I ask you, where are you going to get it?"

"Why won't you help me?"

"If you mean by magically whisking you away to a place where nothing can hurt you, and you'll live happily forever – that's not my job. All I can do is to point you in the right direction."

"Thanks for nothing."

"You're welcome. We'll talk later."

The thought of being abandoned, even by an hallucination, made me panic.

"Wait, at least tell me who you are."

The leaves rustled, and the face looked like it was laughing.

"That would be a long story; I have many names. Let's just say that I protect wild things."

"So why won't you help me?"

"You aren't yet a wild thing."

Table of Contents

The Twelve Steps	1
In the Family Way	9
Wild Thing	22
Duty of Care	35
Doctor John	44
Easily Impressed	53
Sugar and Spice	63

Dedication

For Nikolina, talented actor, paragon of charm, and late adopter of E-books. This one's for you, chicklet.

Other Books by G.W. Renshaw

Stand-Alone Books:

Hic Sunt Dracones: Being a True Account of the Rescue of Professor George Herbert Endeavour from Misadventure

Odd Thoughts

The Chandler Affairs:

The Stable Vices Affair

The Prince and the Puppet Affair
(Coming 2015)

The Twelve Steps

Some people believe that serial killers are just unfortunate souls who experienced poor parenting. If only we had a recovery program for these poor, misunderstood creatures.

Why, Jeffery Dahmer might be walking among us today.

The placard had a floral border, which seemed strange to Rob. It reminded him of the title cards used in early silent films.

The placard sat on an easel, situated to ambush everyone who came down the stairs. Its message was familiar to him:

We admit that we have no power over our urges, and our lives have become unmanageable.

In general he agreed with the principle, although at the moment his own life was more frustrating than unmanageable. He'd been ill for some time, a result of foolishly failing to take advantage of the free seasonal flu vaccination.

The meeting room was remarkably light and cheerful, considering that it was in a grocery store basement. The two walls that weren't covered by a well-executed mountain lake mural were painted a cheerful sun yellow. To his sensitive eyes, it cast a slight jaundice on the meeting. Rows of chairs had been set up facing a podium.

Rob hadn't decided to go until the last minute, and he entered just as the moderator was about to start the meeting. His first impression was that there were an astonishingly large number of people present. He found a seat at the back.

A moment later the man behind the podium cleared his throat, a small sound that nevertheless silenced the residual chatter. Rob thought it was remarkable how the physically small man exuded such a psychologically imposing aura. From what Rob had been told, Brandon was not just the group's leader, he was its founder. Brandon, it was said, claimed to have found inner peace.

Rob was shocked to find himself wondering if a scalpel would reveal the truth of the matter. Despite thinking of himself as creative and intuitive, being so capricious was foreign to him. He also had a prejudice against knives, and a strong conviction that it was wrong – evil – to impose his own choices on another.

"Welcome," Brandon said. "Who would like to start?"

A thin, balding man with glasses tentatively raised his hand. As he moved to the front he reminded Rob of the actor John Fiedler from an old Star Trek episode. The room quieted again as everyone prepared to listen.

"Hi, my name is Phil."

"Hello, Phil," everyone else said, more or less in unison.

"I am a serial killer, but I haven't killed for over three weeks."

There was a scattering of polite applause. Phil seemed to gather his strength to go on.

"My obsession with blonde exotic dancers had gotten to the point where my cooling-off period was only a few days. I knew that the police were closing in. It was probably only a matter of a few weeks at most before I would be caught." He shrugged helplessly. "I was like an addict. I couldn't stop. I was getting sloppy."

He paused, and looked at his audience.

"Some of you may understand what bothered me the most. Not that I would lose my liberty. Not that I would be dragged through the muck of the popular press. What bothered me was that my work would remain incomplete."

Several of the seated people murmured their agreement, including one who said "amen, brother!"

Rob though that Phil was smiling at him. It took a moment for him to realized that he was instead looking at a man seated nearby.

"Then I met Steve. He knew at once what I was, and what I needed. A peer group, people who would understand my problems, and who would help me to achieve liberation."

"All I did was point the way," Steve called out. "You had the courage to walk the path yourself."

"With your help," Phil said to the group, "I have reached step nine in my journey."

There was much more sincere applause this time. Rob had done some research, and knew that for many of them nine was the big one.

"This week I'll be confronting my ex-girlfriend directly. It's time that she paid for what she did to me, and it's time that I make amends to myself for wasting all that time and effort with surrogates."

The applause this time was thunderous. Phil smiled broadly, and raised his fists over his head. Rob thought he looked a bit ridiculous, like the proverbial 98-pound weakling pretending to be an Olympic champion. Phil went back to his seat, several people patting his back as he passed.

A few more people spoke, and Rob sat silently thorough the whole thing. At the end, as juice and cookies were served, Brandon came over to speak with him.

"How did you like your first meeting?"

"It was amazing. I never knew that there were so many of us in one place."

Brandon poured himself a paper cup of apple juice from a box on the table. Rob noted that it was the house brand of the store upstairs. He wondered if their landlord knew what kind of community service group they were hosting.

"It was surprising to me as well when I started the group. We have all kinds here. Some haven't acted on their impulses yet. We hope that our support will help them to avoid any difficulties with the authorities while finding greater satisfaction from fewer projects. We also have some occupational training groups, such as forensic countermeasures, that are very popular. The most popular group by far is on self-understanding."

Brandon looked at Rob, took a sip of his apple juice, and then nibbled on a cookie. It was chocolate chip, also the house brand.

"A lot of us have known for years that we are different, but we don't know exactly how or why. The SU group helps people to gain insight that proves invaluable when it comes to progressing through our twelve steps. Who is your sponsor?"

"Geri," Rob said as he pointed to a middle-aged redhead dressed like a hooker. She was talking to another woman who looked like a suburban housewife. "I was chatting her up in a bar, thinking that she might require my services, but she saw right through me. It was a terrifying moment, but I'm glad I stayed to listen to her."

Rob smiled at the memory. Perhaps Geri would let him help her in turn someday.

"If you don't mind me asking, what is your type?"

"Type?"

"Thrill-seeker, mission-oriented, power-assertive...?"

"Oh, I don't know. Mission-oriented, I guess. I just want to help people."

"Ah," Brandon said, "an Angel of Mercy."

Rob had never thought of himself before in any particular terms, but he felt excitement at the words.

"Yes! That feels right. I can't tell you how wonderful it is to find people who understand."

"That's our mission. I think you might be interested in our methadone program."

Rob was both startled and offended at the suggestion. "I've never taken any recreational drug in my life. I would never cloud my mind that way."

Brandon waived his empty juice cup to brush away the misunderstanding. "Sorry, that's just our nickname for it.

The program provides members with candidates whose lives are arranged to minimize problems. Newcomers can get help with technique, and more experienced members can enjoy an occasional project without fear of complications. Everybody wins."

"That sounds very – appealing. I've been inactive for a few months due to illness, and the thought of all those unhappy people out there... When could I start?"

"How about next week?"

Rob showed up at his appointment a few minutes before noon on Tuesday. He wore his best suit as befit the formality of the occasion.

It was an older neighbourhood. The house was a run down brick two-storey, still sporting some of its original Victorian gingerbread. The boards creaked ominously as he mounted the front steps, and he stayed close to the wall in case the porch collapsed under him.

All he had with him was a packed lunch and a pair of gloves. Brandon had asked about his kit, and Rob was proud to say that he didn't use one. He had a deep respect for his clients, and felt that too much preparation only spoiled the moment. If a person needed his help, they needed to be able to trust him to tailor his services to them spontaneously and effectively.

A minute after he rang the bell the door opened, and a frail old woman squinted at him.

"Good day, Mrs. Pruitt. I've brought your lunch," Rob said warmly. She regarded him with suspicion.

"Where's Sheila? Sheila usually brings my lunch."

"She couldn't make it today. She had some car trouble." He didn't mention that the car trouble involved a jar of honey poured into her gas tank. He thought it fitting that he'd bought it from the same store that hosted their meetings.

Mrs. Pruitt stood looking at him for a moment, then moved aside to let him in. She seemed distracted as she led him into the kitchen.

"I need my glasses," she said, hobbling into her bedroom.

He donned his blue nitrile gloves before searching for her dishes and cutlery. Rob arranged her meal on the plate, and placed it in the microwave oven, looking around while it heated. Kitchens always annoyed him. The sheer number of knives had a tendency to overwhelm his creative process. They made him feel like a painter who opens his box, only to find dozens of tubes of Paris Green on top. He had to dig below the surface appearances. What else was available? What would suit dear Mrs. Pruitt?

He wandered about the room, looking in drawers and cupboards. It was in the refrigerator that he found his inspiration.

Hmm. He estimated Mrs. Pruitt's weight at 45 kilograms. Three syringes of insulin should do it.

She returned, moving slowly and carefully, and sat at the table as he placed her lunch before her. She fixed him with knowing eyes. Somehow, God had made her aware of his Vocation.

"You're here to kill me, aren't you?"

For a moment Rob was taken aback. Although all of his clients asked him for help, this was the first time that one had been so blunt about it. Mostly he got glances, small gestures, minutiae that he had to interpret. It was difficult but rewarding work. He felt that he had to be equally honest with her.

"Yes. I've been sent to you."

Mrs. Pruitt closed her eyes. Her hands trembled slightly, and he reached out to comfort her. She jumped as he touched her, and quickly withdrew her hand.

"I never asked for this."

"God knows your inner heart," he said quietly, "and He told me."

She trembled again, and opened her eyes.

"Will you hurt me?"

"My dear, I would never do that."

She watched with frightened eyes as he revealed the three, 30-unit disposable syringes of insulin he'd prepared along with her lunch. He had no intention of being cruel, and it would be fairly quick.

"Would you prefer...?"

Her eyes never left his hands as he handed the first one to her. She blinked as she took it with a trembling hand, her eyes now fixed on his.

"I don't want to do this," she whispered. "I'm afraid."

"Here, let me help you."

She tried to deny him the syringe, but he easily took it from her. She was so weak that he had no trouble keeping her arms away as he slid the needle beneath her skin and injected the drug. He made little shushing sounds to calm her as she cried out. She was breathing rapidly, and appeared mesmerized by his finger on the plunger. She made no fuss as he emptied the other two syringes into her.

"There," he said when it was done, patting her hand again. "All better."

"Why?" She said in a quavering voice. Tears began to collect at the corners of her eyes. As usual, his vision took on a unique sharpness as he waited.

"I enjoy helping people. In fact, I find it quite exciting, even orgasmic."

Mrs. Pruitt was sweating and her hands were now shaking.

"Do you know where you are?" He asked suddenly.

"What?"

"I'm sorry. That's a problem with drugs. They can spoil the mind's clarity. Oh well, it can't be helped."

She tried to stand, and collapsed to the floor. Her hand reached in the direction of the telephone on the wall. He knelt beside her as she tried to speak, his breath quickening with excitement. He couldn't make out the words but, really, there was only one thing she could be saying.

"You are so welcome," he said happily, stroking her hair.

Over the next few months, in between clients, Rob volunteered to assist Brandon in organizing the group's activities. Rob thought that Brandon was sending him a message, but he wasn't certain. He needed to be certain.

At the end of the second meeting in May, Brandon was moving several boxes of supplies into the back of his van. It was then that Rob received a clear sign.

"Rob, could you help me, please?"

"Certainly, Brandon. All you had to do was ask."

"Good evening, everybody," Rob said at the next week's gathering. "Brandon was called home rather suddenly, and I'll be taking his place. I'll also be implementing some new programs to get people the help they need."

He smiled warmly at his people.

"Who would like to be first this week?"

In the Family Way

If you hadn't noticed, humans are a bit irrational about children.

Rescue personnel will work through a howling blizzard in the dead of night if a child is missing. Women in labour go through hours of pain, and shortly thereafter start talking about having another one. A lot of couples believe that their lives will be just the same after the birth as it was before.

Assuming that she isn't picky, woman who wants children can almost always find a man who is willing to make a seminal contribution to her project.

For men, it can be more difficult.

The people who say "I'm in a relationship, but it's complicated" have no idea. Seriously. No idea.

It was a lovely Saturday in late spring. Michelle was out shopping when I checked the upload progress from my laptop on the kitchen table.

43% COMPLETE.

I puttered around the garden doing odd jobs until I couldn't stand the suspense any longer.

75% COMPLETE.

In desperation, I cleaned the bathroom, did the laundry, and sorted the stuff in the pantry.

87% COMPLETE.

I pulled everything out of the refrigerator, cleaned the

interior, threw out the questionable items, and put the rest back.

95% COMPLETE.

I didn't know when Michelle would be home, so I made lunch and ate it.

99% COMPLETE.

The front door opened, and my beloved entered carrying two cloth shopping bags full of groceries. I got a quick kiss in passing.

"There's more stuff in the car."

I made several trips, lugging a 30-pack of toilet paper, a 20-litre tin of olive oil, and several flats of assorted canned goods. So much for me organizing the pantry. All hail Costco.

"Michelle, I have something to tell you," I said as casually as I could after we'd put the groceries away.

"Sure, whazup?" At work, Michelle was a brilliant, erudite and precise lawyer. When she was at home she tended to be a lot more relaxed about her language. Unless, of course, I was in trouble.

I sat on the living room couch with her beside me.

"Is anything wrong?" She asked.

"No, I just wanted to tell you about my project."

"Finally, the Great Engineer speaks! It's been, what, 16 months since you've let me into the garage. I know that a romance needs mystery, but there are limits. What have you got out there? A better mouse trap? Chained naked slave girls?" I tried not to react but she must have seen something in my expression.

"Jason?"

"Maybe I should just show you."

⤝⤞

The century-old garage at the back of our house was perfect. The paint was peeling off the rotting wooden clap boards, a variety of flora grew on the old cedar shingle roof, and the walls were slightly skewed. The wooden side door had started life somewhere else, and didn't quite fit the opening.

I opened the cheap padlock, revealing a steel inner door. Since Michelle had last been out here, I'd created a second building inside the first. I entered the code to open the inner door, and deactivate the alarm system.

"This is new," Michelle said. And expensive, I could hear her thinking. I'm not generally telepathic, except with Michelle under certain circumstances.

Such as when I'm about to be in trouble.

"Most of it is recycled. You'd be amazed what people throw away. And I did the work myself."

"Why didn't you just tear down the garage, and build a new one?"

"Thieves are very good at cost/benefit analysis. The old garage doesn't look like it contains anything of value."

"How paranoid," she said while looking around the workshop.

We were in the larger of two rooms carefully separated by a heavy plastic curtain. This was the area where I did machining, and other potentially grubby things. The main sound was the bubbling of the 40-gallon fish tank. The other area, currently concealed, was my more-or-less clean room. From there came the muted, incessant whine of the fans for the computer cluster.

Nybbles was sunning herself in the window. She silently jumped from the window ledge to the workbench, to the floor. She trotted over to me, weaving herself between my legs and, bunting me in a satisfied way as Michelle bent down to scratch her behind her ears.

"When did you get a cat, and why is it living out here?"

I took her hand, and guided her back to her feet. "First things first."

When I tapped on the side of the fish tank the entire school wheeled. I pointed out the one with the black, iridescent body. "Michelle, meet Jack. Jack, Michelle."

"Jason," she said precisely, "you just introduced me to a fish."

"Jack isn't a fish. He's a robot."

She gave me the same look I've seen her give to hostile witnesses, and raised one eyebrow.

"I've been working on artificial intelligence."

"So you built an intelligent fish?"

"He's intelligent for a fish. He's a fully functional member of his school. The only difference is that he runs on solar panels instead of food flakes. His neural networks learned how to be a fish by interaction with the others, and that knowledge can be transferred to more advanced robots as a basis for further evolution."

"Interesting." Her tone suggested that this had better be leading somewhere.

I picked up the black cat.

"This is Nybbles."

Michelle stroked her fur again, and then paused with her hand in midair.

"No way."

"Cats like to sun themselves anyway, so it wasn't a big leap to make her solar powered too. Her software is based on Jack's with a mammalian overlay."

"Incredible. She's so life-like. Can you make more like her?"

"Of course. The state of the neural network can be downloaded just like any other software."

"Do you know how much you could sell these for as hypoallergenic non-pets for people whose landlords won't allow animals. You'll make a fortune."

"I already licensed the manufacturing rights to a company in Japan."

She paused for a millisecond, and then became very precise.

"Excuse me? Do you or do you not remember that your girlfriend is a lawyer? Why did you not consult me before signing a contract?"

The secrecy had seemed like such a good idea a year and a half ago. Now I felt like a small child standing next to a broken vase.

"I'm sorry, I needed the money to complete the next steps."

"How much money are we talking about?"

"Um, about $340,000." I saw her eye twitch and hurried

on. "The royalties will generate a lot more over time, of course. Really, that was a drop in the bucket."

"My God, Jason, that would have to be one hell of a bucket. What could you possibly have built that would cost that much?"

Rather than trying to answer I just steered Michelle through the curtain into the clean room.

She screamed.

Not like in horror movies, of course. Just a squeak of surprise at coming face to face with what appeared to be a dead chimpanzee draped over a chair. I'd forgotten about Cornelius.

"You could have warned me. I certainly hope that's another robot."

"Yes, of course. That was stage three. It was difficult getting proper primate behaviour starting with the cat software, but I finally managed it."

She eyed Cornelius with considerable suspicion.

"Why isn't it moving?"

"He's turned off to keep him from wrecking the place. You know how chimpanzees are."

She gave me The Look that said yes, I can well imagine. Then her eyes went past me to the other end of the room and froze. Oh, crap. I should have thought this through a lot more carefully.

One of the equipment trolleys held a keyboard and monitor that displayed a dialogue box reading "Wake? Yes/No." Beside it, on a stainless steel table, was a naked woman. Her eyes were closed, and her chest was quietly rising and falling. A data cable led from her umbilicus to the computer cluster.

"Oh my God, you have been keeping a naked slave girl out here." Her voice became even sharper. "One who looks like she could be my sister."

"She's not a naked slave girl. She's a naked android. That's stage four."

Michelle gave me The Look that said you have ten seconds until detonation.

"An anatomically correct naked android," she said very,

very precisely.

There was no option other than for me to plough ahead and throw myself on the mercy of the court.

"Well, yes, she has to be. Mind can't be separated from its container. That's one reason why every previous attempt to produce artificial intelligence has failed. Ariana is designed to have a human mind, so she needs a human body. She's only a few months old, but she's been interacting with virtual reality at an accelerated rate so that when she wakes up, her development will be somewhere in her late teens. The upload of the neural software into this body finished a few minutes ago."

"Ariana?"

For some reason I felt embarrassed by my choice. "I just liked the name."

"I see," she said with a strong implication that she didn't. "Jason, this is crazy. All that money, and for what? Domestic servants? Sex slaves? I don't get the point of having a fake human female when you are living with a real one."

That was the last straw.

"Dammit, she isn't fake. She's completely real. She's just not organic. Second, this isn't about mass production. I made her because..."

Michelle raised her eyebrow, waiting for me to complete the sentence. Okay, if that's how she wanted this.

"Because you don't want to have children."

It was one of the two times I've seen Michelle confused.

"What does that have to do with anything?"

"I know that your career is important to you, and I would never pressure you to change your mind. But I want a child. A daughter whom I can love, and who will love me in return. I love you, and I don't want anybody else, so I made a daughter myself." I tried to slow my breathing, and my anger exhausted itself. Maybe I could defuse the situation. "Hey, it worked for Zeus."

Michelle didn't smile. She sat on the wheeled lab stool.

"I don't know whether to be proud, horrified, amazed, angry, or just creeped out. I don't want to have a baby so you – made one yourself?"

When she put it that was it sounded so pathological.

"Well, yes. Her facial features are actually a composite of ours, so it looks like we're all related." Now that I was saying it out loud, it really did sound kind of creepy.

"I knew that you were odd when I moved in, but this takes the cake. You have to give me time to process. Suddenly you have a daughter whom I've never met."

"We can fix that. All you have to do is press enter on the keyboard."

"You're kidding."

"Don't worry. It's perfectly safe."

Michelle hesitated for a moment, then reached over and pressed the key. I liked the symbolism of Michelle bringing my daughter into the world.

On the table Ariana's eyes opened, and she reached down to disconnect her cable. Then she sat up, and looked at us.

"Dad?"

"It's okay. This is my girlfriend Michelle."

"Hello Michelle, I've heard a lot about you." She held out her hand. Michelle didn't move. After a moment the hand was withdrawn, and Ariana looked down at herself. "Maybe I should get dressed."

It was obvious in hindsight that I should have dressed her once hardware testing was completed, but after months of working on every detail of her body it just never occurred to me. I kept my eyes on Michelle as Ariana slid off the table, and padded over to the shelf where her clothes were kept. Michelle watched as she put on underwear, a dress, and shoes. I'd included social mores in her education but given that her "childhood" was spent naked on a lab bench it wasn't surprising that she hadn't quite gotten the hang of modesty.

"I'd really like you two to get to know one another," I said. Michelle looked at me with an unreadable expression. "Please?"

"Are you absolutely certain that this is safe? I read science fiction too, you know."

"Completely. Ariana is no different from any other young woman you'd meet. I've tried to make her experience of the world as human as possible. She can eat and drink, although the food isn't processed. She can even have a sex life..." I saw another Look being prepared. "...eventually. If she wishes."

"Daaad," Ariana drawled in the time-honoured way of teenagers.

"This is a lot to take in." Michelle took a deep breath, then blew it out. "All right. Ariana, would you like to go for a walk?"

I saw no reason to create an ugly daughter, and I'd spent a lot of time on facial expressions. When Ariana smiled it was dazzling. "That would be nice. I've never actually been outside."

Michelle fixed me with The Look that said this isn't over. The two women in my life left the clean room, and a moment later I heard the outer door close behind them.

I collapsed onto the stool, pleasantly surprised that I was still alive.

Nybbles bunted my leg and purred.

⌒∽∞∽⌒

Supper time came and went.

I was tempted to call either Michelle, who always carried her cell phone, or Ariana, whose phone was built in. I didn't want to interrupt if things were going well, so I limited my snooping to locating my daughter's GPS. They were in a restaurant about two kilometres from the house. That seemed promising, so I stifled the urge to find out what was happening. Instead, I made myself a sandwich.

It was after ten when they came home. Much to my relief they were chatting and laughing like old friends.

"Did you have a good time?"

"Oh yes," Ariana answered. "Michelle is really fun, and we talked about lots of things. I really like her." Ariana yawned convincingly. "I need to go to bed. See you tomorrow." She headed for the back door. Michelle stopped her with a hand on her arm.

"Don't be silly. You aren't sleeping on a steel table," Michelle said, giving me another Look. "Your father will set up the spare room."

"Cool," Ariana said, giving Michelle a hug, then me. "I'll need an extension cord." The two women went off to arrange whatever else a newly-born teenage android needs for the night.

Later, in bed, Michelle couldn't stop talking about her new best friend.

"She can be very logical. She pointed out that I wouldn't have been able to distinguish her from an organic person if I hadn't known. Certainly nobody we met had a clue. After that we started talking and didn't stop. She has a wicked sense of humour."

"I patterned some of her behaviours and preferences after you."

"You're sweet. By the way, I think you are wrong about her level of maturity. She really doesn't act like a teenager. More like someone my age."

"Yes, 32 is so old." She poked me in the ribs, which led to more interesting things, and then sleep.

⁂

Over the next few weeks Michelle and Ariana bonded like industrial epoxy. Instead of my girlfriend being jealous of the time I spent with my new daughter, I found myself almost having to make appointments to get any time with either of them. The only real limit on their interaction was Ariana's active battery life of 10 hours. She could go almost 30 hours without recharging if she wasn't moving around, but apparently Michelle had taught her to dance. They liked to go clubbing in the evenings.

The time I did spend with Ari was wonderful. She was brilliant (her IQ tested around 160 although I expected that to increase), charming, funny, and loving. She was fascinated by everything, and I finally knew what people with children meant when they said kids make the world new again.

Now that we seemed to be a family I wondered if

Michelle would reconsider getting married. I'd proposed about a year after we met but she was cautious, and wanted to live together first. Five years later she was still being cautious.

After two months I was noticing odd little things. Michelle seemed distracted when we were together. Our love making became less frequent, and she seemed less involved than before. I may be dense, but I began to suspect that she'd met someone, probably during one of their dance nights. My stomach was hosting a Lepidopteran convention, but I had no proof, and I didn't want to accuse her of anything in case I turned out to be wrong.

I casually asked Ari if Michelle had met anyone while they were out, but she said that any social interactions were strictly casual. Several men had tried to pick up one or both of them, but Michelle had taught Ari by demonstration how to cut an unwanted suitor off at the knees. I thought of hiring a private detective to follow Michelle. I hated myself for being so paranoid, then hated myself for being indecisive.

A few days later the matter was taken out of my hands.

I was sitting in my lounger in the living room reading New Scientist when I heard "Jason, I need to tell you something." I looked up to see Michelle standing in the doorway to the kitchen. I put down the journal while more butterflies hatched in my stomach.

"Yes?"

She sat on the couch facing me, perching on the edge with a serious expression.

"Jason, I know that I've been distant lately and I'm sorry. I should have said something before, but I really didn't know how."

"You've met someone," I said. Michelle seemed surprised that I'd figured it out.

"It's not like that." She paused. "Okay, I guess it is like that. The reason I've been so distracted lately is that I'm confused. I love you, but I've also fallen in love with someone else."

Despite my prior suspicions I felt unprepared and light headed. My first thought was that I didn't want Ari to know, then I realized that I couldn't protect her from it. Besides, she was physically and mentally an adult. An ironic thought: Children grow up so quickly these days.

"All right. Given how you've been acting I can't say that I'm surprised. Who is it? Someone from a club? A co-worker?"

Instead of answering, Michelle looked toward the kitchen. Ari came in, sat beside Michelle and held her hand.

"It's me, Dad."

The next thing I knew I was lying on the floor with my head in my daughter's lap. I felt like I was hyperventilating. Tears were falling from Ari's cheeks onto my forehead.

"I'm sorry, Dad. We didn't mean to hurt you. We were talking about sex, and I told Michelle that I didn't think I have any preferences as long as I love the other person. She told me about the girlfriend she'd had for a while in university, and when we compared notes we realized that we're best friends, and we really love each other."

I sat up slowly, and saw Michelle still sitting on the couch.

"Have you slept together?"

"No," Michelle said. She looked at Ariana. "We wanted to talk with you first. It's complicated."

"Dad, I don't want anything to come between us, and Michelle really does love you. She doesn't want to lose either of us, and I don't want to lose either of you. I have a solution if the two of you are willing to listen."

"This is so weird," I said.

"Why," Ariana asked, "because I'm a machine, or because Michelle is human? Michelle and I are in love, and we have sexual needs like anyone else. Dad, I know this isn't a normal situation but it isn't even as weird as Michelle using the toys you bought her. You don't think that's weird, do you?"

"Of course not."

"Toys can't give informed consent. I can."

"All right, what's your idea?"

"Polyamory."

Michelle looked like I felt: confused.

"What are you talking about?" She said.

"Polyamory is the practice of having multiple, simultaneous intimate relationships with the knowledge, and consent, of all involved parties," Ariana recited. I suspected that she was quoting directly from some Internet source via her internal Wi-Fi.

There was silence for a full minute. If you don't believe that's a long time, try it. Michelle had told me about her girl friend in university, so that wasn't a surprise. I tossed Ari's idea around in my head, and discovered that I wasn't horrified. My daughter must be in favour if she suggested it. We just had to convince Michelle. Ariana turned to her.

"I also found a procedural reference from the Usenet alt.polyamory archives. You could have sex with Dad one night, and then just sleep with me. The next night we'd switch the order. That gives each of us three or four nights of sex per week." Despite her intelligence, delicacy was not Ari's strong point.

"Are you seriously suggesting that I hop from bed to bed like a... a..."

"Woman with two lovers?" Ariana suggested. "Yes, why not?"

"For heaven's sake, Michelle," I said, "you're in love with an android. Don't be so conventional. You said that you love both of us. If you and I break up we'd have to sell the house, split our belongings, and do a pile of paperwork. I think it's a workable solution. As long as we're all happy, why not?"

"You'd be all right with this? You wouldn't be jealous?"

"You're the one who's fond of logic. What are the problems with you having an affair? Cheating on me, getting pregnant, catching a disease, not having time for one of us. If we all know and approve, then it isn't cheating. Ariana can't get you pregnant, or give you a disease. If we're all living together, then what's the problem?"

"Strictly speaking," Ariana said, "you wouldn't be having an affair since I am not a natural person in the eyes of the law. Even when you and Dad get married it couldn't be construed as bigamy."

"She's beginning to sound like me," Michelle said. "Wait, when we get married?"

"It seems like the logical thing to do," Ari said. "Ninety percent of couples are engaged for seven to 24 months before having the wedding. You've been living together for six years, which is a statistical anomaly."

"I agree," I said. I looked at Ari, and wrinkled my nose. "Just don't expect me to sleep with my own daughter."

"Eww, gross," Ari said.

Michelle looked more like her old, joyful self than she had for a long time. Her eyes were glistening.

"Are you sure? Both of you?"

Ariana held out her arms to Michelle who was off the couch in an instant to hug and kiss us both. She started crying. So did Ari. For that matter, so did I.

"This is insane but I love you!"

"I love you too," I said between kisses. Ariana's response was muffled by Michelle's mouth but she seemed to agree.

I was feeling completely drained after our emotional roller coaster, but it seemed like we'd reached an elegant solution to a unique problem. The engineer in me was pleased. I also got to keep both the love of my life, and my daughter, and it looked like I was getting married too. Nothing could faze me now.

Ariana pulled back slightly, and then smiled at both of us.

"Now that we've settled that, we should discuss grandchildren."

Wild Thing

We're very proud of our civilization. Most of the time it works fairly well to keep us safe, warm and fed.

Sometimes, though, you just need to go wild.

I tried to be neutral, but my voice sounded bitter, even to me. "So, you never loved me."

Jill shrugged, her hands making vague gestures in the air. The faint smell of her wafted toward me, adding to my misery.

"I'm sorry. You're a wonderful man, but it's just not who I am."

I looked at the packed burgundy luggage by the door; the set I'd given her a year ago for her birthday. They'd been there when I got home from work, and represented the last of what she'd moved during the day. At least she left the sofa.

"What are you thinking?"

I tried to be angry, but I was too depressed to muster enough energy.

"I'm hurt and confused. If you were leaving me for another man I could wonder what I did wrong. Maybe I could do more housework, or read a sex manual to get pointers."

I looked at her. She was waiting for me to continue. At

least she had the good grace to look sad. I let out a long breath.

"None of that matters. I can't match whatever Alison gives you." I paused again. "I thought you were happy."

"I'm sorry," she said gently.

I stared at the floor between my knees while she carried her luggage out onto the porch and closed the door behind her. Two years of my life went with her.

❧

The alarm clock went off at the usual time with all the subtlety of a Michael Bay film. I rolled over onto the empty tequila bottle that almost broke my ribs. On all levels, my experiment to see if alcohol would ease the pain was a complete failure.

It hadn't been a nightmare. There was no Jill beside me in bed.

I managed to get up without further self-injury, and stood under the shower like a zombie too stupid to come in out of the rain. For two years I'd thought of us as more like a single entity than a couple. It sounds trite, but I really felt like half of me was now missing. The other half was on autopilot.

Breakfast was beyond me but I did get dressed, and make it to my car with the idea of going to work.

Like most people, I knew very little about alcohol metabolism. I just assumed that sleeping somehow caused the tequila in one's system to disappear. Fortunately, the shortcut was on a back road. My car was only up to its doors in a bog, not wrapped around a bridge abutment, or another vehicle.

I sat on the shoulder, looking at the car. Green scum and mud caked my legs and trousers up to mid-thigh. At least my mobile phone still worked. One of my shoes was still in the swamp, and the gravel ground into my butt as I sat there waiting for the wrecker. A bubble of air escaped from under the car with an obscene sound, summing up my mood perfectly. Swirls in the algae by my car looked for all the world like a face, laughing at me. I gave it the finger.

The face didn't seem to care.

The wrecker finally arrived, and the driver was – wait for it – Jill's brother. We said as little as possible to each other as he dragged my Toyota out of the swamp. Of course it wouldn't start. He offered to tow it to my mechanic for a substantial fee. There wasn't much choice.

He made me sit on some rubbish bags while I was in the cab so I wouldn't get the seat dirty. Apart from me giving him directions, we said nothing to each other.

Adding insult to an estimated three thousand dollars worth of injury from the mechanic, I had to walk home. The wrecker had left. Neither the taxi nor the bus wanted me, covered as I was with stinking mud. I limped along making squishing noises with every other step. My skin itched where the mud was drying.

I could have sworn that I saw the same green face looking at me from a tree. As the leaves moved gently in the breeze it looked like it was laughing. This time I ignored it. Maybe I was going mad. All I wanted was to go home, take another shower, and try to figure out how to live without Jill.

⤙⤚

The old industrial park was home to a variety of wildlife, from legitimate workers, to the homeless, to prostitutes, and drug dealers. Going through it would shave at least an hour from my walk. It seemed like a good choice at the time. I guess a lot of things do.

The filthy, homeless man who popped out of the doorway of an abandoned building must have thought I was a brother. His face was weather beaten, his teeth were bad, and he had a bottle of cheap whiskey in his hand. He probably smelled, but I really couldn't tell over my own eau de bog. The weirdest thing was that he looked familiar, despite having flowers and leaves stuck in his hair.

"Spare change?"

I assumed the head-down-keep-going posture of a city dweller trying to ignore a beggar. My unshod foot found a sharp pebble, and I tumbled to the ground with a cry of pain. When I looked up he was kneeling by my head waving his bottle at me. Yes, he stank like a barnyard.

"You want a snort?"

With all that had happened, and the smells, my stomach rebelled and I threw up. My new friend sat beside me, unconcerned, swigging from his bottle.

"She isn't worth it."

It took a while for his words to penetrate.

"What?"

"Jill. She isn't worth it. She knew what she was before you even met. You owe nothing to someone who lied from the start."

"How the hell do you know what I've been through?"

He took another drink from his bottle.

"I know a lot, even here."

There was something wrong with this conversation but my brain wasn't even close to working properly.

"Leave me alone." I remembered Jill's smile back when I thought we were happy, and my misery hit rock bottom. "I'll never find anyone like her again."

"If you're lucky," he said, nudging me with his bottle. "Did you know that she hooked up with you on the rebound from another woman? She actually believed that sleeping with a man would punish her ex." He laughed. The sound was oddly like branches of a tree knocking together in the wind.

He prodded me with the bottle again. "You're too close to the problem right now. Never make a life-changing decision while you are in pain."

"Says the guy who lives in a doorway." At that moment, lying on the ground, caked in mud, and my own vomit, I really wanted to die.

"Suit yourself, but be careful. It's Friday."

"What does that..." I looked up but he was gone, probably back to his hole to drink himself to death. I wondered if all homeless alcoholics were therapists. How did he know about Jill?

My brain was still on autopilot, and wanted to go home. I struggled to my feet and began walking.

The metal grate was level with the pavement, one of those mysterious installations with no visible purpose that dot every city. From the depths issued the subdued roar of something mechanical.

It all happened so fast. My stockinged foot stumbled on the grate, and I pitched forward toward an open hatch. I fell through the hole, and smashed into what felt like branches. There was a sharp crack, immense pain, and I passed out.

At some point after that, I suppose, I must have hit bottom.

I awoke several hours later, lying on a bed of gravel at the bottom of a concrete shaft. The good news was that I was no longer drunk. The bad news was that I hurt all over, the hatch looked to be about six metres above me, and I was no longer drunk. My forearm throbbed. When I tried to move it, there was a searing pain and a grating feeling.

Years before, a random seed must have blown down the shaft, and an ash tree had taken root in the dirt at the bottom. It had broken my fall, and my arm, on the way down. I'd snapped off a fairly large branch that was now under me. I carefully sat up, and leaned against the cold concrete. My arm ached like a bad tooth. According to my watch, it was about four P.M. I tried to wait until I stopped shaking, but then I retched again. Have you ever tried to throw up when even breathing sends jagged flashes of pain through your arm? I passed out.

It was now after six. "Help!" I yelled as loudly as I could, every few minutes until my throat was sore. As the homeless man had reminded me, it was Friday. Any workers would be at home by now and I'd have to wait until Monday – no, Tuesday, Monday was Labour Day – to be rescued.

I fumbled for my mobile phone inside my jacket. It wasn't there. Far overhead I saw a dark rectangle lying on the grate.

I passed out again.

It was dark. A dim, wire-caged electric light in the shaft shone down on me, and my first coherent thought was to wonder why would anybody waste the electricity here.

I looked around my new world. Miscellaneous junk littered the bottom of the shaft. I was lucky that I hadn't been impaled when I fell. There were two big, round ducts in one wall. Warm air was blowing from them. In another wall was a steel door. Starting about two metres from the floor, metal rungs were set into the concrete below the hatch.

When I looked at the tree, my illusory, leafy friend was back. The features reminded me of the homeless man. The whole situation pissed me off.

"What are you looking at?"

He didn't reply. It would have been the icing on the cake if he had.

I managed to shuffle over to the steel door that I'd seen earlier. It was locked. There wasn't even a proper knob on my side, just a finger tab below the key hole.

More shuffling took me to the nearer duct. Behind it I could hear some kind of machinery but the grate was solid, and there was no way I could budge it with one hand.

I looked at those ladder rungs on the wall. Maybe I could reach them somehow.

I could, but didn't have the strength to pull myself up with one arm. There was nothing I could stand on. I tried using the tree, but it was impossible to climb with my broken arm.

I sat down by the wall. There was no way out, and I was convinced that I was going to die here. Given my life on the surface, that didn't seem so bad.

⚮

The voice was like the one from the burning bush in DeMille's *The Ten Commandments*. At first it was so soft that I didn't know whether I could hear it, or if it was in my head. It gradually increased in volume until I could make out the words.

"Are you happy now?"

"Help!" I screamed. Obviously someone was nearby on the surface. "Help me! I'm trapped in the pit!"

When the reverberation died away there was silence. I kept yelling for about 15 minutes. There was no reply. Then the voice came back.

"That's a lot of effort for someone who wants to die."

"Where are you? Please, help me!"

"Why don't you help yourself?"

"I can't. I'm hurt." I was starting to sound like a whiny five-year old, but I couldn't help it. "I need help."

"You certainly do. Where are you going to get it?"

I looked around but couldn't see anyone. Movement in the tree caught my eye; the leafy face was back. The mouth seemed to move in synch with the words which seemed only slightly peculiar at the time. I thought, how can the leaves be moving if there's no wind? I must have been delirious. Maybe it's not just those who have been manhandled by Orcs who think that talking trees are normal.

"Please, I need help."

"So you say. Again, I ask you, where are you going to get it?"

"Why won't you help me?"

"If you mean by magically whisking you away to a place where nothing can hurt you, and you'll live happily forever – that's not my job. All I can do is to point you in the right direction."

"Thanks for nothing."

"You're welcome. We'll talk later."

The thought of being abandoned, even by an hallucination, made me panic.

"Wait, at least tell me who you are."

The leaves rustled, and the face looked like it was laughing.

"That would be a long story; I have many names. Let's just say that I protect wild things."

"So why won't you help me?"

"You aren't yet a wild thing."

⌘

Time passed.

More time passed.

My whole body ached, and there was no position in which I was comfortable for more than a few moments. My watch said it was 8:17 on Saturday evening. I was hungry, and I tried to remember how long someone could live without water.

"Are you still here?"

I was sitting against the wall dozing when the voice jerked me awake.

"I have to get out of here."

"You'll get no argument from me. How are you going to do it?"

"I don't know. I need help."

"No, you don't. What you need is to stop thinking of yourself as a poor, wounded little beast, and start thinking of yourself as a Lord of the Forest."

"I don't want to be Lord of the Forest, I just want to go home."

"Then you have a problem. You can't have one without the other."

"There's no way out."

"An animal in a pit says there's no way out. A Lord of the Forest makes a way out."

"What the hell does 'Lord of the Forest' even mean?"

"When you are one, you'll know."

I thought about what the voice had said, even though I was pretty sure that it was all in my head. I'd tried everything, hadn't I? I couldn't reach the ladder. The door was locked. The grate over the first duct was solid. The second duct was – untried.

The second duct's grate seemed loose. I pulled on it with my good arm, causing pain to lance through the other. I managed to brace myself better for the next pull but it still hurt.

The next hour was spent pulling the grate, resting, pulling the grate, and resting. After a while it seemed to be moving further which was encouraging.

With a screech of rusted metal, the grate suddenly swung outward. It caught me by surprise, and I fell backward onto my arm.

Guess what? I passed out again.

∽

The sky was beginning to lighten when I awoke. As long as I didn't move it, my arm merely ached, but my back and head hurt where the gravel had gouged me during the night.

The duct cover was still open. Inside was the sound of machinery, a breeze and darkness. I needed to do something with my arm so I could crawl through.

There was an old, plastic shopping bag among the rubbish. I tore the plastic with one hand and my teeth to enlarge the handles, and slid them around my neck. That formed a perfect sling for my injured arm, and I managed to button it inside my jacket. My arm was as protected as it was going to get.

The duct went in about four metres, and then gently curved to the left. The wind was blowing in my eyes, and I had to squint. In the semi-darkness I almost ran into the fan with my face.

In films, fans in air ducts always rotate so slowly that you kind of wonder why the hero doesn't just walk between the blades. These were whipping around like a normal fan. I doubt that anyone could have thrown a pebble through without it being chopped in half.

I crawled back to the pit. A few hours ago I might have just sat there, now I wondered what else I'd missed. Despite the hunger and thirst, my mind seemed to be functioning more clearly than it had since Friday morning.

What did I want? What did I have? What did I need? I needed some way of getting past that fan. Maybe I could use something to jam it.

The branch that I'd broken on my way down was at least ten centimetres across at the base. It was heavy as hell, and took a long time to move, butt first, into the duct. The side branches seemed to catch on everything, and there were only so many that I could snap off with my one good hand.

Once it was in position I had to crawl back out so I could push it into the fan. I didn't want to be anywhere close to those blades when I shoved a big stick into them.

I sat there breathing for a while before I grabbed the branch, and braced myself as well as I could.

Everything happened at once. The branch slid forward. There was the terrific noise like being inside an industrial wood chipper. A loud bang was followed by a continuous screeching sound like tires on pavement. The branch twisted out of my grip, and threw me against the side of the duct where my arm exploded with pain.

I lay there panting for several minutes while my body swore at me. At least I didn't pass out this time. The screeching continued, and I could smell burning rubber. Nothing else seemed to be happening.

It took me a long time to crawl in past the branch. It had jammed the fan blade very nicely. The screeching was coming from the fan belt that was still trying to turn the blades, and the air was hazy with acrid smoke. Lying on my back, I pushed myself through head first with my legs. There was another grate, but mercifully it swung open when I bumped into it. I pushed hard, and promptly fell on my head.

When I regained consciousness yet again, I was on the floor of a room filled with machinery and very little light. I managed to get to my feet, holding onto the wall with one hand. In the distance an exit sign glowed red. I was very cautious as I made for it, not wanting to trip over anything. It only took me half a dozen rest stops to get there.

The door was locked. Feeling around, I found a light switch beside it on the wall. The fluorescent lights made me blink as they came on, illuminating a slight blue haze in the air from the smoking fan belt. They also showed me a washing station a few metres away.

Housekeeping was obviously not a priority for whoever

worked here. I couldn't have cared less. The dirty, industrial sink had functional plumbing that included the most delicious stale, tepid water I've ever tasted.

I think I drank three litres, one cupped handful at a time. I didn't know if that was a good idea in my condition but, again, I didn't care. There was a primal joy in slaking my thirst at the water hole.

Now that I could properly see the door, I found the knob for opening the deadbolt. The door opened onto a flight of stairs with another steel door at the top.

The feel of natural wind and sun on my face was indescribably wonderful. Maybe I was a Lord of the Forest after all. My next step was to get home.

The police car slowly drove into sight at the end of the building, closely followed by an ambulance. They were the most beautiful things I'd ever seen.

"Congratulations," a voice said behind me, "you saved yourself. I thought you deserved a reward."

It was the homeless man, still garlanded with flowers and leaves, and carrying my mobile phone. I swayed back and forth on my feet, and he helped me to sit against the door jamb."I don't think you should mention the tequila when you tell them your story. Good luck." He dropped the phone on my lap.

The constable got out of her car and came over to me while her partner kept watch.

"Sir, we're responding to a nine-one-one call. Do you need help?"

"Yes," I said far more weakly than I thought I should and turned my head. The homeless man had disappeared again. When I turned back the paramedics were coming toward me with a gurney. I let myself be taken to hospital.

⚬⚬⚬

Three weeks later when my door bell rang. The caller was not who I expected.

"Hello, Miles," Jill said. She looked nervous.

There was a flutter in the pit of my stomach, then a flash of anger and then – nothing.

"Yes?"

"Could I come in?"

"Why?"

She burst into tears.

"Oh Miles, I'm so sorry. I made a terrible mistake and I was wondering if... if..."

"You want to get back together." I was amazed at how calm I felt. I idly scratched at my arm where the cast was irritating it.

"Please, I'll do anything. I'm so sorry I hurt you. It was all..." She was almost incomprehensible through her tears.

"A terrible mistake?"

She sobbed even harder, and sank to her knees. I sighed.

"Come in."

I gently closed the door behind her.

"Sit down," I said, indicating the sofa where I'd sat three weeks before. I sat in the chair facing her, watching her cry until she got hold of herself.

"Thank you for seeing me."

"I didn't do it for you. My neighbours don't need the trauma of wondering why someone is sobbing and screaming on the front step. I take it that Alison didn't work out." She burst into tears again, and I waited until the storm abated.

"Do you see a pattern here?" I said. "A woman breaks your heart, and you run to a man to get even with her. Another woman breaks your heart, and you run back to the man. Are you trying to get even with Alison now?"

Jill looked at me as if I'd caught her in some secret perversion. In a way I had.

"No, it isn't like that. I... how did you know?"

"What was her name; the one before me?"

Her shoulders slumped forward and her eyes wouldn't meet mine.

"Marisa."

"I'm sorry, Jill, but you need to figure out what you want before you get into another relationship. Until that happens you'll keep bouncing back and forth, being miserable and leaving a trail of misery behind you."

"But I love you."

"No, you don't. A wise man made me realize that you just love being in love. Otherwise, you'd have asked about my arm."

If I'd been in a vindictive mood the look on her face would have been priceless. She was so self-absorbed that she honestly hadn't noticed my cast before I mentioned it. I stood up and opened the door.

"Goodbye, Jill. I hope you find what you need."

After she left I went for a walk. Regardless of the insights I'd gained over the past few weeks, the whole visit hurt a lot. I wondered if I should try to find the homeless man and have a talk.

I was walking past a church when I saw him. Right there, just behind a statue of Mary, carved into the stone niche, complete with the crown of leaves and flowers.

"Thank you," I said to the carving, feeling slightly foolish. A light breeze touched my cheek, and I heard a tinkling sound reminiscent of laughter.

It was probably the bamboo wind chimes by the church door.

Duty of Care

The people in emergency services - police, fire, EMS, and SAR - deal with the unthinkable on a daily basis. The toll it takes on them as human beings can be greater than most people are able to imagine.

Some can't take it, and I have nothing but respect for the people who get out before it destroys them. I often wondered what might happen if they didn't.

By the time I woke up I was in the kitchen, my fingers on the speed dial and speaker phone buttons. The pager that had roused me continued to sound until I silenced it while the phone dialled the emergency message centre. My uniform was kept neatly folded by the phone, and I pulled it on while waiting for the recording to begin.

"Westmore Search and Rescue, April 13 at 0525. We have been called out to search for a 14 year old female missing in the area of Bridgeport Park. Meet as soon as possible at the park office, and bring your swift water gear."

I wrote down the details, not that I would ever forget, and ran for the garage in my socks, hitting the remote start and garage door buttons on the way past. As the door lifted, and my truck roared to life, I took a few precious seconds to re-confirm that the storage box in the bed was properly loaded before taking off. That was paranoia. The box is always loaded and ready to go.

Bridgeport Park was only about six kilometres from my house, and I had the most efficient route memorized. Nine minutes after my pager went off I pulled into the parking lot. I would have made it in eight, but there was a cop lurking near one traffic light. I didn't dare run it. I had to sit there, cursing at the delay. It's stupid that the police consider search and rescue to be civilians. They are allowed to drive as fast as they want in an emergency. Why can't we? At least stopping gave me a chance to pull on my boots and lace them. Doing that while driving is a skill I've had to develop on my own since nobody else seems to care.

There were a few vehicles outside the park office, all police and park officials. I was the first searcher on the scene. Again.

I parked, grabbed my rescue pack from the passenger seat, and my swift water gear from its niche in the storage box. I was inside the office and filling out the sign-in sheet before the cop lounging behind the desk could move. He was starting to open his mouth when Constable Callaway poked his head out of the meeting room. We'd worked together before. He was good. He looked around and sighed.

"Are you the only one here?"

"Looks like."

He sighed again and muttered something that sounded like "oh, great." It must be difficult for him to work with people who aren't as dedicated and professional as I am.

"Okay, come on through," he said.

I dropped my gear by the desk, and entered the inner sanctum. Some people were talking on phones, while two search managers quietly argued over a large scale map covering the table. One guy was writing a time line on the white board. I never told anyone, but it always gave me a rush to see search base at work. This was the Mind of the operation, just as we field personnel were Its Senses and Hands. Search and Rescue: the Eyes and Hands of God.

Callaway led me over to a quiet corner.

"We need as many three-man teams as we can put

together," he said. "The centre of the old foot bridge washed out late last night, and our preliminary investigation shows the subject trying to wade across at 0220." I shook my head. Wading across the river would be difficult at the best of times, let alone in the middle of a flood. "I'll have the briefing ready in about 10 minutes."

I gave him a curt, professional nod, and left to do my job. On the way out I grabbed a two-way radio and extra battery pack from a box by the door. I also noticed a couple in their forties, holding hands and sitting in the corner looking frightened. A female constable was interviewed them. Obviously, they were the subject's family.

In the outer office, more self-proclaimed searchers had arrived, wandering around and chatting aimlessly. "Outside, now," I barked. Some of them gave me a dirty look, and I heard someone say "him again" but I didn't care. I get results.

Once outside, I led the herd away from the building so we'd be out of earshot of any other family members who might be around. I did a quick head count. At this point, half an hour after the call out, we had only 17 people. Pitiful.

"Sort yourselves out into three-man teams. The radios are inside. Meet back here for the briefing within 10 minutes, ready to go. Be aware that the subject's family is in there, so watch your mouths. Karen and Jaime, with me."

Karen Reid is the best tracker I've ever met, period. Jaime Myers has eyes like a hawk, and is a crack radio operator. I wanted both of them on my team. In five years I'd never failed to bring back a subject, and I wasn't going to start now.

"I have a present for you," I said to Jaime as I handed over the unit and extra battery. He stepped aside to do a radio check. I love working with professionals.

"What's the story?" Karen asked. I told her what I knew. A couple of teams were starting to wander back when another Conservation Officer came out with a stack of paperwork for us.

We recorded who was on which team, then Karen took the list into the office while I skimmed the top information sheet. When she came back I began the briefing.

"Listen up, people. The subject is Misty Morgen, a 14-year old Caucasian female." *God*, I thought, *what a name. Some parents should be shot.* "She is 5 foot 5 in height, 125 pounds with long red hair. After spending most of the night at her friend's house she left to go home around 0200. At 0220 the friend received a cell phone call from her reporting that her normal route home, the old park bridge, had partially collapsed but that she was going to attempt a crossing anyway. The friend's father and brother then wasted an hour looking for her before calling the police. When last seen she was wearing a red sweater, t-shirt, blue jeans and running shoes. She has no known allergies, and is apparently not on any medication. Questions?"

"Any domestic or psychiatric problems?" Someone at the back asked. At least one of them was paying attention.

"None that we're aware of. Any other questions?" I paused for a moment. "OK, team leaders pick up your information and search assignments. Remember, we've had two weeks of rain so the river is fast and dirty. Be careful out there."

Four more people had arrived so I handed out the search assignments for teams Bravo through Golf, reserving team Alpha for myself.

Alpha's search area was just downstream from the bridge in the highest probability area. Jaime drove us down the service road while I looked over the documentation again. It was then that I finally got to the back where her photograph was.

I knew her.

I hadn't known her name before, but I'd seen her around my neighbourhood. She was sweet, and innocent-looking, and incredibly beautiful. The kind of beauty that makes you want to do nothing but stare at a girl for hours.

Now, don't get me wrong. I'm no pervert. I'd never tried to speak to her, but I liked to watch for her after school. I'd smiled at her a few times as we crossed paths on the street, and she'd smile back. I think she knew how I felt about her. I had to save her.

I *would* save her.

We parked near the bridge, and I surveyed the river, reading the current. The normally quiet water was a surging, frothing mass of brown filled with logs, broken branches and miscellaneous junk. If Misty had gone into the water, where was she now? Caught in that strainer? No, the current would have swept her past it. Downstream I saw what looked like an eddy. Could she have been caught there? Swept back toward shore? That was the best bet.

"We'll start at the far end of the area," I said as we shouldered our packs. I looked at the sky. The sun would be up in a few minutes.

We had to move far more slowly than I wanted. The area was flat and normally it was covered with grass, some shrubs and a few trees. Now the water had receded somewhat, but parts of it were still flooded. The vegetation was knocked flat, and was a muddy, tangled mess. Assorted junk from upstream, mostly bushes and trees, made the going even slower.

Every few minutes we called Misty's name. There was no answer.

I was almost frantic by the time we reached the eddy, but I couldn't let it show. The muddy water swirled slowly around in a vast circle maybe 15 metres or more across. There was a lot of debris bobbing around that Misty could have used to get herself out. We spread out, only three metres apart so we wouldn't miss anything, and started to walk the shoreline.

"Here," Jaime called after about ten minutes. He was hunkered down beside a muddy bank, and he pointed to some marks as Karen and I approached. Jaime and I stood back while Karen went into tracking mode. When she gets like this it's almost like she's channelling spirits.

"Somebody crawled out of the water here. One shoe, probably a runner. The shape of the foot is probably female, about size 6. She scraped her knee on this rock."

Karen moved slightly. "She rested here for a while, the mud is compressed." Karen touched the mud with her finger tips. "About three hours ago. Went that way." She pointed at a game trail through the bushes that led toward the bridge.

Jaime radioed the information back to base as we took off with Karen on point. We lesser mortals flanked her a few metres apart and further back in case something got past Karen. Fat chance. We were calling Misty's name every half minute or so as we went. I found a shoe just as Karen called a halt.

"She's stumbling from side to side, cold and hurt. Tripped over this log and fell flat on her face. You can see the chin and hand impressions and some blood. She knelt here a while, then moved on without her remaining shoe."

"I found a fresh runner a few metres into the bush," I said. "She must have thrown it." I held the shoe in my hand reverently. Misty's shoe.

"That's not good," Jaime said. "I've heard of people who are hypothermic or dehydrated removing clothing. For some reason it makes sense to them at the time, but it's usually fatal."

"That's not what we have here," I said. "She probably just found it awkward walking with only one shoe." I couldn't picture Misty doing something stupid.

"I hope you're right."

We moved a bit quicker as the light increased. The coating of silty mud on everything made the track almost too easy to follow. Visions of finding Misty, cold and hurt but essentially unharmed, swam through my mind. I would pick her up in my arms. Triumphantly carry her into search base. She would be smiling with her head resting on my chest. Her hero. Right now she was probably sleeping somewhere under a bush or tree.

The tracks stumbled through puddles, and kept fairly close to the river. When we reached the paved main trail the tracking got much tougher. We'd been following Misty for almost 40 minutes. Karen studied the pavement, then walked slowly, still following the signs.

The track led through another mud puddle and then onto the bridge. None of us could find tracks leading away again.

This wasn't possible. Nobody would have tried to cross again after being swept away once. I stared at the bridge, trying to find some other explanation, while Karen and Jaime stood there watching me.

"Art," Karen said quietly. I admit it, I jumped at the sound. "It's pretty clear what happened."

"No," I said firmly. "We just aren't reading the clues correctly."

"She tried to cross the river, lost her footing, and was swept down stream," Jaime said. "Between being cold and hurt she made a bad call, and tried it again." He looked like he was going to cry, and cleared his throat. "I don't think she was lucky twice."

"No," I said again. "If she went in again then she'd be caught in the eddy again. Radio base and bring them up to date. We're going to go back to the eddy and search again."

I caught a look between Karen and Jaime as I took off downstream. I didn't care. We'd wasted too much time as it was. After a moment she followed me, and I could hear Jaime talking on the radio behind us. All of my attention was focused on that sweet girl who was out here somewhere waiting for me to rescue her.

Seven hours later we were called back to base. We'd looked everywhere something the size of a teenage girl could possibly be. We'd examined every stick, stone, and patch of mud for clues. We'd found nothing beyond our original set of tracks.

Maybe she'd been swept further downstream before she got out this time. She could have been picked up by someone, taken to a clinic that hadn't gotten around to telling anyone yet. She was alive. I could feel it.

When we got back to base we heard that her sweater, torn and muddy, had been found caught on a bush three kilometres downstream by team delta. There was no other sign of her yet. The current must have pulled her sweater off before she got to the eddy. It didn't mean anything.

For the next several days I spent every waking moment combing the area for some sign of Misty.

My boss is a bastard. He left a bunch of messages on my answering machine, asking when I'd be returning to work. As though Misty's life didn't matter. Finally he left a message telling me not to bother coming back. It doesn't matter. I've never left a subject behind, and Misty needed me.

⁂

It's been five days. The initial search day was the only one when it hasn't rained. I tried searching at night but I just can't take the chance of missing something. When I finally go to bed I dream that I can hear her calling to me to find her.

Karen came by early this morning. Caught me just as I was leaving. Says she's worried about me, and asked when I'd last had a bath. I told her to worry about Misty instead. She said that Jaime thinks I'm too obsessed about this search. I told her that they could either help me, or get out of my way. I'm disappointed. I thought they understood.

After seven days I heard on the ten o'clock news that they officially called off the search. Her parents thanked everybody for their efforts, and I threw the can of beans I'd been planning to have for supper through the TV screen. Murderers, all of them. Misty was out there waiting for us to find her.

I called Callaway to give him a piece of my mind. To get him to do something. You know what that ass hole said? "Art, you've always been obsessive, but now you need to get professional help." Can you believe it? What a jerk. That's what I'm trying to do! These people are supposed to be professionals. Why won't they help me find Misty? I have to waste time travelling to and from the park because they won't let anyone stay there overnight. I've gotten a couple of speeding tickets. It pisses me off when they waste my time like that, but if I try to explain it to them it just takes longer.

Misty is calling to me, but I can't quite reach her.

There's this connection between us. I know that if I could only figure out the clues, I'd find her and bring her home. I know now that the dreams aren't just dreams.

I decided to write this journal, to document my search for Misty when everybody else has given up. I might as well use the time I'm forced to spend away from the park for something useful.

Twelve days. My head has finally cleared. I realized what it is that I've been missing. I feel like an idiot. It's been right in front of me the whole time. I know how to find her. All I have to do is to go back to the bridge, and follow her down the river.

If I leave now I can reach her before dark. I'll complete this journal when I return.

I can hear Misty telling me to hurry.

Doctor John

In the 1960s, one of the greatest hits of the folk group Peter, Paul and Mary was Puff the Magic Dragon. *Despite rumours to the contrary, it is not a drug song. It's about the lost innocence of childhood.*

It's also about personal betrayal.

The sweep second hand of the wall clock in the engineer's booth slogged its way uphill to touch the twelve as Keith watched. At the touch of a button, brash, jazzy theme music launched itself through the air to blast from the radios of the station's faithful listeners.

"What do you get when you cross Doctor Phil with Rush Limbaugh? The Doctor John Show!"

The music came up, and ended after another few seconds. The voice over continued.

"Welcome to another edition of our show, in which noted psychologist Doctor John Popierius tells it like it is while our callers reveal their innermost secrets."

In his isolation booth, John congratulated himself. He'd always hated his stupid birth name, and using Google Translate to find a cool-sounding equivalent had been an act of genius. Of course it meant that he had to invent a Lithuanian ancestry for interviews, but...

"And now, here's Doctor John!"

Keith pointed at John through the window.

"Thanks, Keith," John said in the rich, authoritative tones he'd paid his voice coach a fortune help him develop. "It is usual for therapists to concentrate on the traumas of childhood because past traumas cause current distress. Tonight we'll be doing something a little different, exploring your dysfunctional childhood dreams to show how the dysfunctional youth becomes the dysfunctional adult. Our society idolizes the dreamer, from the capitalist entrepreneurs of the early Industrial Age to the Man of La Manchu's 'To Dream the Impossible Dream' to Martin Luther King's 'I have a dream' speech. But are dreams the stuff of life, or do they cause life to get stuffed?"

A yellow light was flashing on the telephone line selector, and he poised his forefinger over the matching button.

"I see that we already have a caller. Go ahead, you're on the air."

He pressed the button.

"Hello, Doctor John?"

"Hi," he said, "what's your name?"

"I'm Monica. I'm not sure what you mean about dysfunctional childhood dreams. When I was five I wanted to be just like ballerina Barbie, and I don't think that I'm dysfunctional now."

The woman's voice pegged her as a whiner who just wanted him to refute what she already knew about herself. Excellent. People like her kept his ratings up.

"In what way did you want to be like Barbie?"

"You know, all tall and slender. And I wanted to be a dancer."

Oh, this was going to be good, he thought

"I see. May I ask, what are your height and weight now?"

"Uh..."

"Come now. If, as you say, you aren't dysfunctional, then surely you aren't sensitive about your appearance."

"All right, fine. I'm five foot three and 180 pounds. But most of that weight is from the stress of my job."

The whine was starting.

"Which is?"

"I'm the wardrobe mistress for a local ballet school."

"Just to be clear, you aren't a dancer yourself?"

"Well, no."

"And how does that make you feel?"

There was a pause.

"I'm okay with it," Monica said. He could hear the slight tremor in her voice.

"You don't sound very okay."

"I'm fine. Just fine." Her voice was definitely quivering now.

He pushed the button to mute the call so she couldn't interrupt him.

"Let's talk about Barbie dolls for a minute. The average American girl under eleven owns ten of them. Each one is stacked like the cards in La Vegas: If she was a real woman her waist would be something like 18 inches. Parents don't realize how damaging these things are to young girls – girls who see Barbie as an impossible role model for beauty when their own genes will make them short and obese. On top of that is Barbie's complete lack of sex organs with all the gender-shame and confusion that this creates. It's no wonder that we see all kinds of psychological conditions caused by these horrid travesties of humanity: Frigidity, depression, borderline personality disorder, obsessive-compulsive behaviours. Some girls have been known to become suicidal because they can't live up to the standards of Barbie and her ceaseless, vapid smile." He unmuted the call and heard sobbing. "So, Monica, how long have you been working at the ballet school?"

There was a slight click, and the yellow light went out.

"Monica? Too bad, it looks like she hung up. Let's pause for a break and then take more calls."

The On Air light over the window went out, and Keith's voice came through with a flat, filtered sound. They really had to get the station owner to spring for new headphones.

"Nice one John. If we don't get mobbed by irate seven-year olds, or sued by the toy company, that should be worth a few rating points."

John reached surreptitiously into his jacket pocket, hoping that Keith wouldn't notice.

"I do it all for you, Keith. Man, I can't believe that loser. I wonder if she's ever gotten laid?"

"Are you volunteering?"

John carefully took a cigarette out of the pack and found his lighter.

"Forget it. I prefer my women like my cars: fast and not in need of an overhaul."

Keith laughed, and John took the opportunity to light the cigarette.

"John, how many times do I have to tell you? You can't smoke in the studio. Besides, those things are going to kill you."

John turned his head and blew a long cloud of smoke over his shoulder, avoiding the microphone in front of him. Keith was so uptight about his equipment.

"Whatever you say, but it won't be cigarettes that kill me. I plan to go at the age of 100 while screwing three other men's wives."

Keith snorted. "Is that your dysfunctional childhood dream? Dump the cigarette, we're coming up on the end of the commercial. Ten seconds. Five... four... three... two... one..."

John carefully ground the glowing end against the cigarette pack.

"And we're back with another caller. Go ahead, you're on the air."

"Hello, Doctor John."

He felt a shock. It wasn't the words, and the voice didn't seem familiar. It had a curious quality to it: cultured, patient and subterranean. Somehow he knew that the speaker was someone who has gone through great pain, and found purpose on the other side. Maybe it was the way the caller emphasized his title. Whatever. Crazy. He shook off the mood.

"Hi. What's your name?"

"Don't you recognize my voice?"

The caller spoke in slow, measured tones, as if to an idiot child.

"No, have we met?"

"Oh yes." There was a pause. "We've met."

There was dead air for several seconds. John had to fill it. Silence was not good radio.

"Well then... What was your childhood dream?"

"I never had a childhood. I just shared one."

This guy's completely nuts, John thought. This will be great.

"I'm sorry, I don't follow."

"No, I don't suppose you would, Doctor John. I've been watching you for years, and you don't get much, do you?"

John's feeling of alarm was back. The callers were his prey, not the other way around.

"Are you stalking me?"

"Oh no, John. Not in the way you mean. I've come to pay you back for the way you ruined my life."

"O-kay. I think we'll take another break now." He pushed the mute button but the yellow light stayed on. He made a frantic "kill" gesture to Keith who did something with his console, then spoke through the headphones.

"There's a problem. He's still connected, and you're still on the air."

"You can't hide, Doctor John," the caller said. John could conceive of this being the voice of a serial killer. He could picture this voice sadly and patiently explaining to a bound victim why God had told him that they had to die horribly. "I won't let you hide. Not any more."

"Who are you?"

"You really don't remember, do you? The sailing ship? The kings? The pirates?"

Keith's voice came over the headphones. "John, we can't kill the transmitter either. Everything is going out live." He sounded frantic.

"Look," John said, "I've never met a king or a pirate, and sailing makes me sea sick. You have me confused with someone else."

"Oh, I don't think so. Can you imagine what it's like to have your best friend betray and abandon you? Can you imagine losing everything that gives your life meaning? Can you imagine sitting alone for years, longing for death but unable to die? Can you imagine, Doctor John? Or doesn't your famous empathy stretch that far?"

John had a sudden, horrible insight. This wasn't just another angry caller he could play with. It wasn't Monica crying because John had been mean to her. This was a person who completely believed that John had done something so heinous that the only sensible response was to hate him with a total purity of emotion. This was hatred beyond the reach of rhetoric, anger or any chance of reason. The hatred defined the caller, just as faith defined the Pope. Perspiration dotted John's brow and he felt nauseous. It took him a moment to find his voice, and as he spoke he knew that his only chance was to fight back.

"What are you talking about?" John asked.

Keith's voice came to him again over the headphones. John jumped at the sound.

"John, I've called the police. Keep him on the line long enough for a trace."

"It was autumn. There was mist that night. A cold, grey mist. I waited by the sea for you – and waited – and waited. But you never – came – back."

"You're crazy, I've never lived anywhere near the..."

"I was your best friend, and you never – came – back."

"Where was this? Maybe if you give me more details I can remember."

"Nice try. I know about the phone trace, John. It won't do any good. They can't trace calls from the lower world."

At last. The caller had given him something to work with.

"Lower world? Do you mean Hell? Is that where you think you are?"

"You slept through most of your anthropology elective, didn't you, John? The lower world isn't anything like Hell, except for me. Do the terms totem or power animal mean anything to you?"

"Of course I'm familiar with the terms, but I'm not sure how they're relevant to your situation."

"Come on, Jackie-me-boy. Even you must realize that they're relevant."

My God, John thought, how long has this wacko been stalking me, and why?

"Nobody's called me Jackie since I was a child. Is that when you think you knew me?"

"Oh, I knew you, Jackie. Remember when you were five and had measles? I nursed you back to health. Remember the pneumonia when you were seven, and stupidly went out to play in the winter without your coat? I cured that too. I was exhausted for weeks after that one."

"How do you know about my childhood? Who are you? Were you a friend of the family?"

"I'm sure you'll figure it out – eventually. Just before I pay you back for decades of misery."

"Maybe if you described yourself I'd remember."

There was another long pause.

"I'm not sure you're ready for that."

"Try me."

"So, the brave Jackie surfaces again. All right, it's your funeral."

Keith's voice broke in.

"John, they can't trace the call. The police are coming to protect you until they catch this guy."

"They'll never catch me, Keith. Only those in the upper world can do that, and even if they interfere it'll be far too late for Jackie-boy."

There was a sudden release of tension as John realized what was happening. The caller was psychotic and resourceful, but there was nothing at all supernatural about him.

"Gotcha! That's how you know what my engineer is saying to me." John laughed like someone who realizes that what he thought was a terrible monster in the woods at night is just a plastic bag caught on a tree. "You have the studio bugged, don't you? I'll bet there are cameras as well."

The caller's laugh was a bubbling, chthonic sound. A fumarole might have laughed like that.

"I don't need cameras. I'm inside your head, John. But don't get all warm and comfortable about it. I'm real, not a psychotic delusion. Ready for that description now?"

John caught himself starting to hyperventilate. He'd dealt with a lot of crazy people in his career but this guy was too creepy for words.

"Jackie? Don't die on me yet. I want you to come to full realization first."

John felt himself spinning completely out of control. Who was this guy?

"Uh…"

"Let's see, I have brown eyes, and what I'm told is a cute nose. I'm about 20 feet tall, with lovely iridescent green scales, and a muscular tail. I can probably still lift you with it, even if you have turned into a pudgy bastard who smells like a dead ashtray. I haven't had much call for breathing fire or roaring lately, but I bet that I've still got it. Sounding familiar yet?"

The implications struck John's reason, and swept it away in a torrent of adrenaline. He gasped for breath and his heart raced.

"No – I never told anyone…"

"That's right, Jackie. You never told anyone about me."

"But it can't be! Puff wasn't real. You – he was just an imaginary friend."

"What do you think totems are, Jackie? I was your friend and your protector. When you went away it nearly killed me. Or it would have if I could die." Incredibly, the voice became even more sarcastic as it mocked his psychological tag lines. "How does that make you feel, Jackie? How's that working for you?"

"This is impossible," John whispered.

"That would be the denial phase."

"Please! What do you want?"

"That would be bargaining. Too bad you won't get to the acceptance phase. It's time to wrap up this show. You broke my heart, now I'm breaking yours. Say good night,

Doctor John."

"Wait, I... oh – God..." A crushing pain slammed into John's chest, shooting down his left arm, and up into his jaw. He couldn't get air into his lungs, and as the vice tightened his eyes widened in agony and terror. Through the window Keith could see John's mouth work soundlessly. A second later he fell forward onto the table, bumping the microphone before sliding noisily to the floor.

"John? John, what's wrong?" Keith's tinny voice sounded from the headphones that now lay by themselves on the carpet. Radio listeners heard the sound of the isolation booth door opening, then muffled footsteps.

"John!"

There was a pause while Keith knelt to check John's pulse.

"Oh, my God."

From the caller came a deep sigh of contentment and satisfaction.

"Thank you, Jackie Paper. This has been a real healing experience for me."

The phrase "easily impressed" is pretty common. I'd heard it for years without thinking much about it. Then one day this story jumped into my head. At least now it's out, and without having to resort to brain surgery.

I hate having to resort to brain surgery for stories.

After fourteen hours on the move, Alonso Heth's legs had long since passed through the towns of Tired and Aching, and were on their way to Numb. Adding to his fatigue was the necessity for constantly watching the road in front, behind and overhead. As well he knew, helicopters could sneak up on you in an instant.

Gravel crunched underfoot as he stumbled along. Otherwise the surrounding forest was quiet. He hadn't seen any signs of humanity for several hours. He needed to start thinking about food, water, and somewhere to hole up for the night. The daylight was almost gone when he caught a brief flash of light visible through the trees.

Jackpot.

There was no fence along the road to provide a clue of where the driveway was, and he almost missed it. It was overgrown, and the deep ruts were full of water from that afternoon's rain. He followed the track carefully, trying not to leave any obvious traces where he left the main road.

The house, hidden a few dozen metres into the trees, was badly in need of paint. The roof, still covered by antique cedar shakes, supported an impressive variety of plant life. A verandah with rotting Victorian gingerbread ran around the two visible sides, and the stereotypical, rusting carcass of a 1940s Ford truck sat among tall grass in the yard. Brilliant light shone through lace curtains from a window on the ground floor. It reminded him of the gas lanterns they'd used in Afghanistan.

On the verandah, an ancient man was sitting in a rocking chair. He had a blanket covering his knees. His face was thin, and he looked as if a breeze would blow him away.

Al sauntered up to the house in his most friendly manner.

"What can I do for you, young fella?" The man said in a voice that matched his appearance.

"My car died a couple of kilometres down the road. I was wondering if there was any chance of me finding a place for the night."

The old man rocked a few times, looking at Al, then nodded.

"I think that could be arranged. Why don't you sit for a while, then join us for supper?"

He indicated a second rocking chair. Al climbed the steps and sat heavily. Damn, not moving felt good.

"My name is Don Moore," Al said, extending his hand.

"Shelby Meadows," the old man said, shaking the offered hand. The handshake was as feeble as Al had anticipated. If it came to it, he probably could take this guy with a harsh look.

"I appreciate your hospitality," Al said as he massaged his aching calves.

Al was trying to think of a way to find out how many people were in the house without raising suspicion when Meadows spoke.

"My daughter – Mariam – and her daughter – Suzi – are taking care of me. It's just the three of us." There was an odd rhythm to the man's speech, a tiny pause before each name as if he was trying to remember them. Or maybe making them up.

A few minutes passed while Meadows rocked and Al rubbed. The only other sounds were the crickets, and the occasional soughing of wind through the trees.

"Have you been walking far?"

"There aren't many rides around here."

"People are leery of picking up strangers, what with the prison being nearby."

"Really?" Al said.

"About fifty kilometres from here. Just about as far as a fit escapee could walk in a day, if he was smart enough to avoid being caught."

If Meadows hadn't been looking toward the road as he spoke, Al would have suspected that he was fishing for a reaction. Perhaps Meadows was just being garrulous. Heth had seen no sign of power, a satellite dish or television antenna as he approached the house, and cable TV was just about impossible this far toward the mountains. It was unlikely that Meadows had seen anything on the news about the escape. Radio reports were another matter, but radio couldn't show his picture. Nor did anyone but him and the man he'd killed and robbed know what he was wearing. Fortunately, the cop had civilian clothes in his car.

"This would be a funny place for a convict," he said. "I'd expect someone to stay near a highway, and try to make it to the city instead of heading out here."

"That depends on how smart the convict is," Meadows said, "Most head for the city and that's where the manhunt concentrates. A clever man would do the unexpected. A really clever one would plan on crossing the mountains on foot. Living off the land. Nobody would be looking for him on the other side, and he could go anywhere."

Holy crap, Al thought. Either this guy is a mind reader or...

"You sound like you've had military training," Al said carefully. "Where did you serve? Korea? Vietnam?"

"In – another – war," Meadows said.

This is not good, Al thought. The old guy was probably former special forces; a normal soldier wouldn't be coy about stating where he'd served. Al had been hoping to spend the night, pick up some supplies, and be on his way without any complications. Despite his willingness to do what was necessary, he didn't kill if he didn't have to. That might not be possible now.

Al occasionally glanced toward the road hidden by the trees. There was no sign of headlights in the gathering darkness.

"Expecting someone?" Meadows said suddenly.

"No," Al said, "I'm just impressed by how quiet it is around here."

Meadows chuckled.

"Most people don't even know we're here. Still, we impress more people than you'd guess."

Before Al could reply to this the front door opened. Meadow's daughter was a relatively plain woman in her forties with brown hair, although she looked pretty good to Al after a nine-year enforced abstinence. Maybe he'd have to look into that before he did anything permanent. Under her red gingham apron, her dress looked like it had been bought that day, but the style was old. Al wasn't an expert in women's fashions, but he guessed that it would have been stylish in, what, 1920? Were they in some kind of religious cult?

"Supper's ready," she said in a flat voice. She showed no surprise that there was a stranger sitting on the verandah. Maybe she had mental problems. That wouldn't bother Al. He'd done worse things in Pakistan.

Despite his age, Meadows stood up without apparent effort. Al was the one who had to lever his stiffened muscles out of the rocking chair.

He expected the inside of the house to be as shabby as the outside. Instead it looked like a set from a Victorian film: dark wood antiques, lace doilies, floral wall paper, and oval-framed pictures of people long dead. Many were dressed for the 1800s. A few were wearing even earlier costumes. That bothered him for a moment. As far as he knew, there were no cameras in the 1700s. Maybe the pictures were of a costume party, or maybe the cult just liked old clothes.

The antiques alone must be worth a fortune. The illumination was provided by real gaslight. That was just weird. Domestic gas lighting hadn't been used for, what, 100, 120 years? The good news was that all of this made it unlikely that these people had a computer, and it made it more likely that he'd have other things that Al could use while he put his army survival, evasion, resistance and escape skills to the test.

The meal was already laid out on the dining room table, and Meadows insisted that Al sit at the head. Suzi, the granddaughter, appeared to be about ten or so with a marked resemblance to her mother. Most of Al's experience with children had been in third world areas where many of them carried weapons. Suzi's overly serious expression made him nervous.

Al wasn't sure what he was expecting, but the food pleasantly surprised him anyway. Baked ham, peas, potatoes with parsley and freshly baked scones. He would have bet money that there would be apple pie for dessert, and he dared to hope for old cheddar with it instead of ice cream. He loaded his plate.

"What do you do, Mr. Moore?" Mariam asked.

"I'm a security consultant," Al said between mouthfuls. Damn, this woman could cook. He hadn't had anything like this for over nine years.

"What does a security consultant do?" Suzi asked.

"A lot of different things. Mostly I keep my clients safe. Won't Suzi's father be joining us?"

"Suzi doesn't have a father. Do you find the work satisfying?," Mariam said.

Al took a forkful of ham, and chewed slowly to give himself time to think.

"Very," he said once he'd swallowed.

"You must have a lot of interesting skills," Suzi said.

Al didn't say anything. He just nodded his head as he

ate. Where was this going?

"I'd like to hear what they are," Mariam said as she put another piece of ham on his plate.

"I'm not sure that's a suitable topic for the dinner table," Al said with a pointed look at the girl.

"At a minimum, you'd be proficient in evasive driving, small arms use, unarmed combat and surveillance," Suzi said. "Anything else?"

Al was becoming concerned, but he couldn't figure what was going on. If they knew who he was they'd be stupid to say anything that made him suspicious. If they didn't, why were they asking? Meadows seemed to be concentrating on his supper, leaving the interrogation to the females. He'd seemed chatty outside so that was strange unless this was an interrogation. Surely they didn't think that the three of them could take him? Hell, in Syria he'd taken out four Mossad operatives who got in his way with nothing more than a knife.

"What do you do?" Al asked. "Farming?"

"We're with the Press," Meadows said.

"Local newspaper?"

"Not local, no." Mariam said.

"Do you have skills with improvised munitions?" Suzi asked.

Al dropped his fork.

"Please forgive Suzi, Mr. Heth. Delicacy isn't her strongest attribute."

Al exploded backward from the table, standing as his chair tipped over. Before it hit the floor he'd drawn the cop's pistol stuck in the back of his jeans.

"Hands on the table! All of you!"

All three of his hosts serenely complied. There was no sign of any panic, or indeed any emotion at all.

"There's no reason for you to be upset," Suzi said.

"We aren't going to turn you in to the police," Mariam added.

"Yeah, right. Where's your telephone?"

"We don't have one," Suzi said, "we've never had a need for it."

"Radio? TV? Computer?"

"No, nothing like that," Mariam said.

"Then how did you know who I am?"

"We read your mind," Suzi said. "Unfortunately, we can't get all the details we need that way."

"Stop that!"

"Stop what?" Mariam said.

"Stop talking in turns!" Normally he was the calm one, and the people he was pointing a weapon at were the ones who were freaked out. He looked at the girl.

"You, stand up slowly, and tear strips about six inches wide from the table cloth. You're going to tie up your mother and grandfather. If you try to run or attack me I'll shoot them."

"Go ahead," Suzi said in a perfectly normal voice.

"What?"

"Although attempting to coerce me by threatening my putative family members is usually a viable tactic, you should know that it won't work in this case."

"All right, Miss Smart Mouth, I'll shoot you instead."

Suzi shrugged. "Be my guest."

"Do you think I'm joking? You have no idea who you are dealing with."

Al kept most of his attention on the two adults, expecting some reaction. Apart from breathing, and occasional blinking, both of them were eerily still. Neither seemed to care that their lives were in peril.

"All right, forget it. Give me the keys to your car."

"We don't have one," said Mariam.

"Your truck, then."

"The only truck on the property is the one outside," Meadows said. "It doesn't run."

"I don't believe you. You have to have some way of getting into town. ATV? Motorcycle? Horse? Bicycle?"

"No," Mariam said, "we don't have any of those."

"We don't have anything you can use," Suzi said.

"Bull," Al said, "You must have something: money, tools, weapons, food, backpack."

Meadows nodded toward the table. "This is all that's

here."

"I'm not stupid. You can't live out here with nothing."

"You're making the assumption that we live..."

"You didn't answer my question," Suzi said. "What other skills do you have?"

Al's life had been filled with people trying to kill him, so he was very good at reading the ones who actually stopped to talk first. As far as he could tell, his hostages honestly didn't care what he did to them. They also truly believed that they had nothing that he could use to aid his escape.

He didn't have time for this. If they knew his name they must have some kind of communications gear. That might mean that the police were on their way. He couldn't take the chance.

"You want to know about my skills? Seven years in special forces, three of them in counter-terrorism. Five years as a mercenary eliminating people for whoever paid me. I've killed more people than you've met in your life so you do not want test me."

"But we have to test you. It's our job," Mariam said.

The deadpan delivery shocked Al out of his anger, and he realized what was wrong. He'd met a lot of people in his profession, some of whom were bug-house nuts, and got a big giggle out of killing. Others viewed death, including their own, the same way normal people thought of trimming their toenails. What were the chances that he'd stumble onto an entire family of psychopaths?

"I think we've seen enough," Meadows said. He looked at the other two and they nodded slightly.

"Don't," Al said, moving his finger from the guard to the trigger.

"We'd like to offer you a job," Mariam said. "You'll be paid very well for killing."

This had to be a delaying tactic.

"Forget it. There's no way on Earth I'm falling for whatever you're trying to do. Kid, tie them up."

"We never said the job was on Earth," Meadows said.

"If you won't volunteer, then we'll just have to impress you," Suzi said as all three of them stood.

"Sit down," he said, taking a step back. "I don't impress easily."

Suzi reached down to pick up the carving knife.

The pistol spat fire and thunder. A red splotch appeared on the girl's chest, and she fell forward, the knife clattering on the wooden floor. The adults didn't move.

"Very good," Mariam said calmly. "You are even willing to kill children if they threaten you. We need more people like you." The adults turned toward him in unison. He'd seen a lot of weird shit overseas, but these hicks were seriously creeping him out. He wondered if it was just cult brainwashing, or whether they were on drugs as well.

"Stay where you are!"

"We're leaving now." Meadows said.

There was a moment of disorientation as Al's vision blurred. Shit, had they drugged him too?

He had to act before whatever they'd given him took effect. Al shot the old man, then the woman. Just to make sure he shot each of them again in the head as they lay on the floor. In Tajikistan he'd learnt fast that it paid to be certain.

The wooziness passed as he searched the house. Every drawer and cupboard was empty. There were no utensils in the kitchen; the refrigerator wasn't even running. He tried the oven. Like the refrigerator, it was a dead prop. The rooms upstairs were completely empty. Not even furniture. As they'd said, the food and knives on the table were the only things of use.

That, Al thought, was enough of that. He went to the front door, and threw it open. He took exactly one step onto the verandah before he stopped dead.

Instead of dark forest and starlight he was nearly blinded by artificial light. When he stopped blinking, he was looking at the inside of a huge, brilliantly lit, hangar of some sort. He could see several other houses identical to this one and things moved among them.

His brain started at what the hell are those? Then it jumped to animals?, followed closely by animals don't wear clothes. The creatures had six limbs, and alternated between walking on the back four, and standing on the back two. The front two sets seemed to be hand-like, with the middle set being more muscular. At first he couldn't figure out which way was front, until he saw several coming toward him. The confusion was caused by the second pair of eyes in the back of the head. Their faces made the unmasked predator he'd seen in that Schwarzenegger movie look as cute as a kitten.

For most of Al's life he'd been in situations where hesitation meant death. He took in his surroundings for maybe two seconds before retreating back into the house. If none of the things had spotted him, he'd have at least a few minutes to figure out how he got here, where here was, and how he was going to get away.

He was looking out the window when he felt a hand on his shoulder. He spun around, pistol at the ready. Suzi, the bullet hole still in her chest, was standing beside him. Behind him were the other two. Where their heads had met the bullets there was a glint like metal.

"We told you that we'd impress you. There's a war on, and the Khairti need experienced soldiers."

Meadows and Suzi grabbed his arms. No matter how hard he struggled, they had no difficulty in marching him out the door to meet his new employers.

Sugar and Spice

Some people say that the internet is brimming with evil predators who are just waiting to pounce on every child who goes anywhere near a computer.

Just remember that every ecosystem has an apex predator.

Beyond the reach of search engines, in the dysphotic realm of the Deep Net, a group of men met to discuss their interests.

Loliluvr: Does anyone know what happened to teddy357?

Girl4me: dunno. cops??

Loliluvr: I didn't see anything in the news about an arrest.

Lolipop: Maybe the parents caught him.

Girl4me: sux 2 b him

Lolipop: Sucks to be you if you aren't careful. How's your project coming?

Girl4me: redy 2 meet

Emmaline and Cindy-Lou were twin sisters, with curly blonde hair, and big blue eyes. They preferred to wear the same outfits, and their most favourite outfits consisted of the cutest little saddle shoes, knee socks and powder blue jumpers with pink ribbons around their waists.

The other children sensed a strangeness about them, and so the sisters got picked on a lot in school. It didn't seem to bother them. The girls just stared coldly at the bullies until they gave up. It's no fun to torment someone who never cries.

When the girls were seven a boy tried to beat up Emmaline. He didn't see Cindy-Lou until after she had grabbed his ankles from behind, timing it so that he stumbled as he moved forward. His nose and three teeth broke when he hit the ground. His ribs broke when they both kicked him over and over and over again. Neither of them said a word during the whole incident. Neither of them showed any emotion at all.

They didn't have any trouble with bullies after that.

When they were nine, a nice police officer came to the school to tell everyone about perverts. Perverts, they were told, were a lot like bullies but worse. The girls knew what to do about bullies. How hard could it be to deal with perverts?

The twins' father was frequently out-of-town on business, and their step-mother was more concerned with her career and social life than with the extra-curricular activities of the two odd girls she'd inherited.

That was good.

It gave the girls a lot of unsupervised time and, although their mother didn't know it, kept her alive.

Cindy-Lou found out about the Deep Net, and was having lots of fun exploring it. It was a fascinating place where you could find all kinds of fun and interesting things.

The girls spent a lot their spare time swimming around in the Deep Net, learning the details of how perverts worked.

Their first project together had been teddy357. She had found him in a chat room called SWEETI-MEET, and for months she let him believe that he was grooming her, telling her how nice she was and asking for pictures. She played along, not fooled for an instant. Bullies that pretended to be friends were old news to the twins.

When the time was right, she agreed to meet him after sunset in a park near their home. She watched as he scouted the whole area before approaching, wary of traps but finding nothing. He saw a darling little girl in a blue dress who was waiting for him by the public washrooms, her hands folded in front of her. She was just as cute as her picture. She smiled and giggled and gave him her hand so he could lead her inside.

The screams went on for a long time, but on that side of the park there was nobody close enough to hear them. It was terrible; the girls got blood on their favourite dresses, and had to wash them when they got home so they wouldn't stain.

⌒⊶⌒

Their next project went by the screen name girl4me. They shared the task of grooming him for almost six months, never telling him that there were two of them. It was fun that he tried to pretend that he wasn't nervous, but when Emmaline sent him pictures of herself he relaxed and they set up a meeting.

The long time between projects might have been boring but the girls kept themselves entertained by playing with fires. And puppies. Sometimes both together.

This time Emmaline stood outside while Cindy-Lou waited inside. Cindy-Lou was wearing old clothes that she didn't care about, and when girl4me came into the building with her sister he had no idea what hit him. It was their father's aluminum baseball bat. Daddy always said that the right tool made a job much easier.

Perverts and fire were even more fun than puppies.

⌒⊶⌒

Beyond the reach of search engines, in the dysphotic realm of the Deep Net, a small group of men met to discuss their fears.

```
Loliluvr: There are some really sick
people out there. Now I know how black
people felt in the fifties. Why can't
```

they just let us live in peace?
   Tinytot: At least nobody's burning a
cross on your lawn.
   Loliluvr: I'd prefer that to whatever
happened to teddy357 and girl4me. I
haven't heard from Lolipop in a while
either. I'm afraid to go to sleep.
   Sugardad: We're being persecuted for no
reason.
   Tinytot: It's not fair. We love little
girls, we don't hurt them.
   Loliluvr: I just don't feel safe
walking down the street any more. Little
girls scare me.
   Tinytot: We shouldn't talk about this
on line. You never know who's listening.
Let's meet in person to discuss about how
to protect ourselves.
   Sugardad: That's a good idea.

❧

After the last response on the screen, Emmaline turned
to her sister.
   "Do you think they'll all come this time?"
   Cindy-Lou thought very seriously for a few seconds.
   "I think we need another baseball bat."

About the Author

G. W. Renshaw is a writer, martial artist, Linux druid, and actor who lives in Calgary, Alberta, with his lovely wife, and the twin cats Romulus and Remus. He has a wide range of interests, from flint knapping to quantum cosmology. He will happily watch just about any film with tentacles in it.

You can connect with him at:

Twitter:
www.twitter.com/GWRenshaw

Facebook:
www.facebook.com/pages/GW-Renshaw/
287045931461429

Website:
www.gwrenshaw.ca/

www.ingramcontent.com/pod-product-compliance
Lightning Source LLC
Chambersburg PA
CBHW032124050726
47590CB00008B/2952